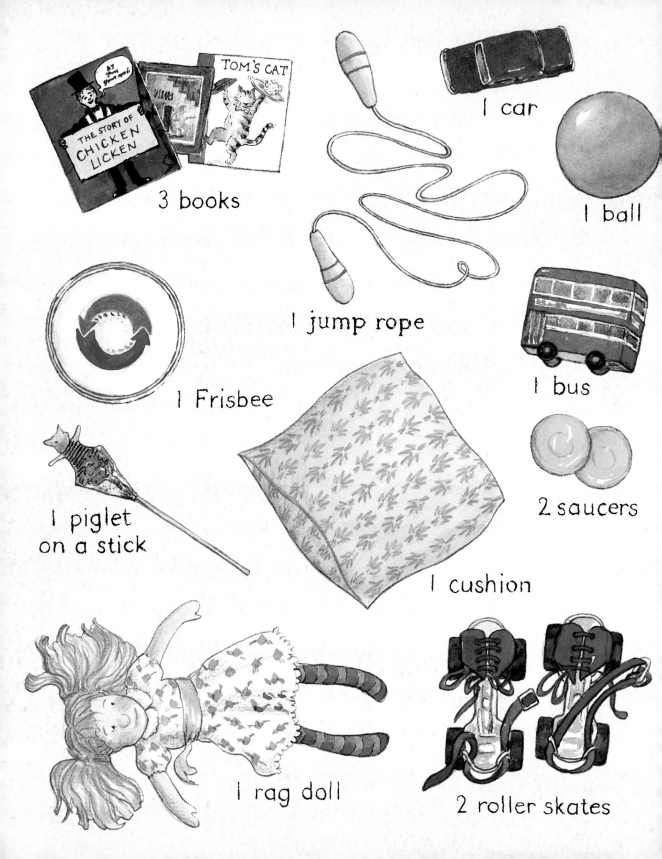

3 books

1 car

1 ball

1 jump rope

1 Frisbee

1 bus

2 saucers

1 piglet on a stick

1 cushion

1 rag doll

2 roller skates

2 blocks

1 ruler

1 dress

1 telephone

1 yo-yo

1 rabbit

2 cups

1 jigsaw puzzle

1 quilt

1 teddy bear

1 teapot

For Leanne and Nathan

Bet You Can't
Copyright © 1987 by Penny Dale
First published in England by Walker Books Ltd, London
All rights reserved. No part of this book may be used
or reproduced in any manner whatsoever without written
permission except in the case of brief quotations
embodied in critical articles and reviews.
For information address J.B. Lippincott Junior Books,
10 East 53rd Street, New York, N.Y. 10022.
Printed and bound by L.E.G.O., Vicenza, Italy
10 9 8 7 6 5 4 3 2 1
First American Edition

Library of Congress Cataloging-in-Publication Data
Dale, Penny.
    Bet you can't.

    Summary: At bedtime, a sister and a brother engage in
a bout of challenges as they tidy up their room.
    [1. Bedtime—Fiction.   2. Brothers and sisters—
Fiction] I. Title.
PZ7.D1525Be 1988   [E]   87-3780
ISBN 0-397-32235-6
ISBN 0-397-32256-9 (lib. bdg.)

BET
YOU CAN'T

WRITTEN AND ILLUSTRATED BY

Penny Dale

J. B. Lippincott   New York

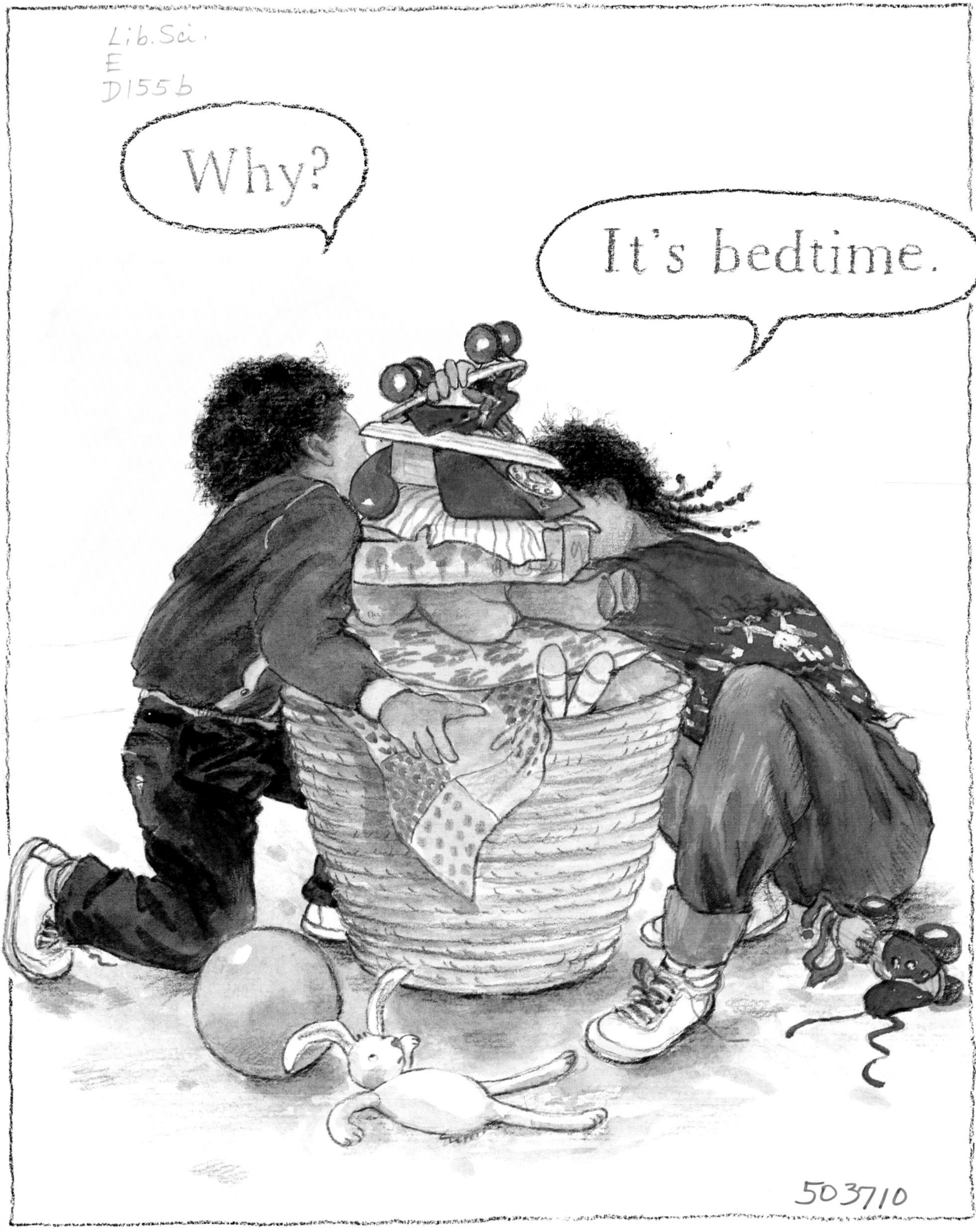
Why?
It's bedtime.

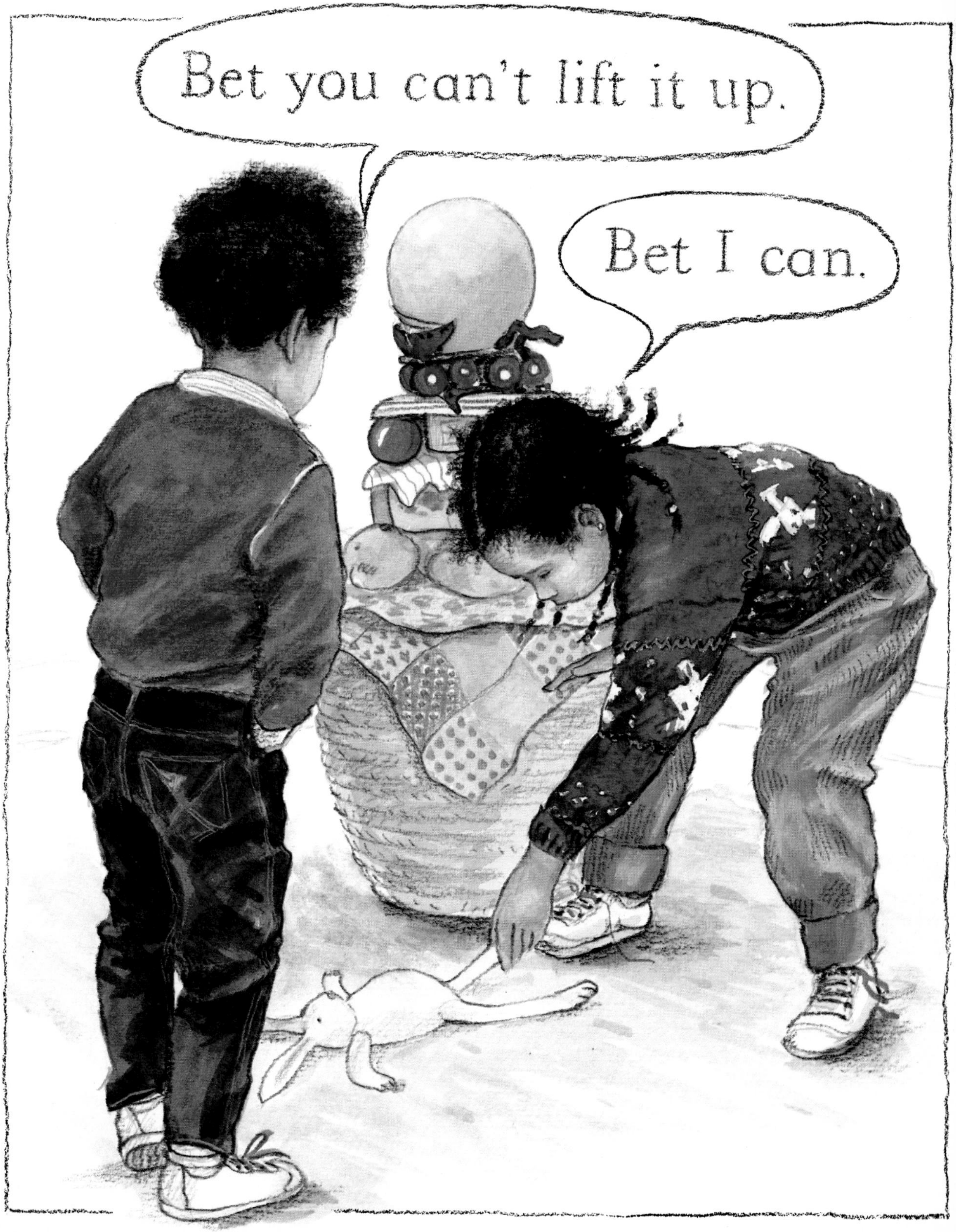
Bet you can't lift it up.
Bet I can.

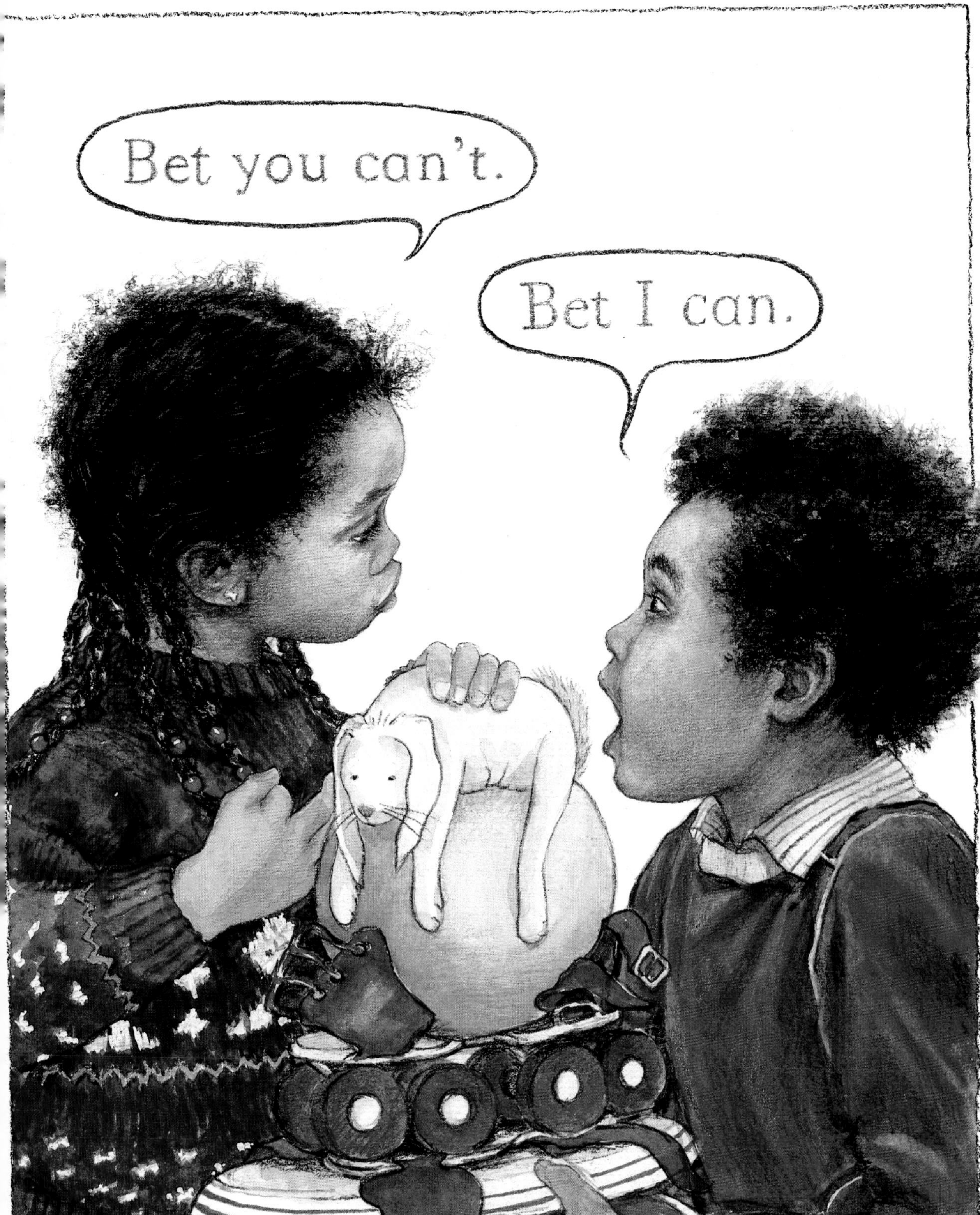
Bet you can't.
Bet I can.

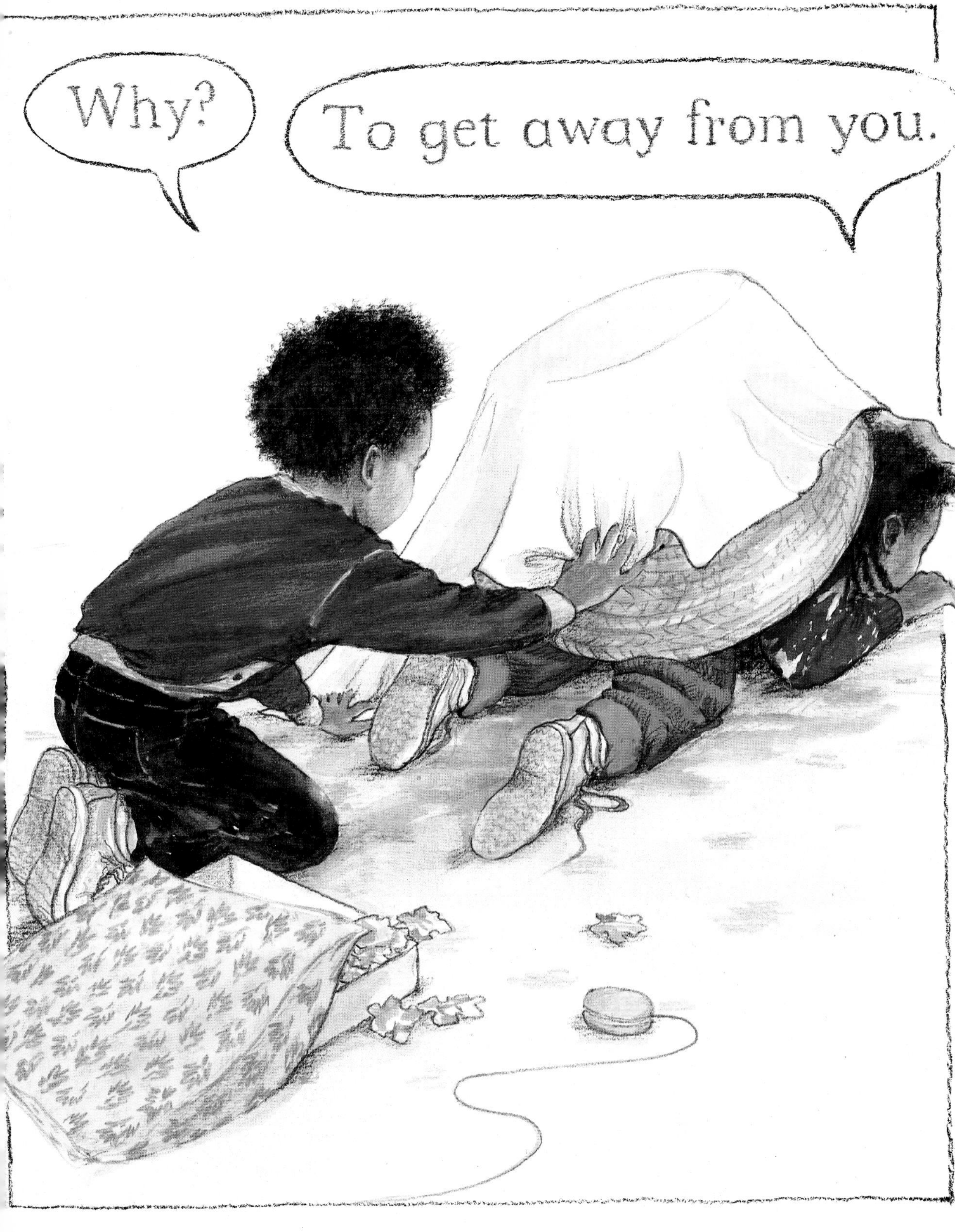

Why?
To get away from you.

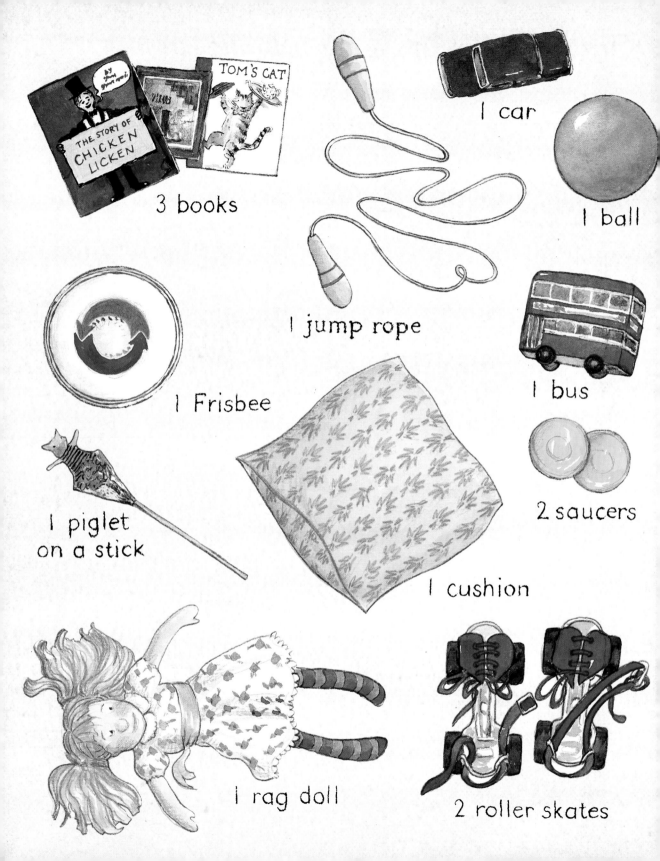

THE STORY OF CHICKEN LICKEN

TOM'S CAT

3 books

1 jump rope

1 car

1 ball

1 Frisbee

1 bus

2 saucers

1 piglet
on a stick

1 cushion

1 rag doll

2 roller skates

2 blocks

1 ruler

1 dress

1 rabbit

1 telephone

1 yo-yo

2 cups

1 jigsaw puzzle

1 quilt

1 teddy bear

1 teapot